THE Seventh UNICORN

The Five Mile Press

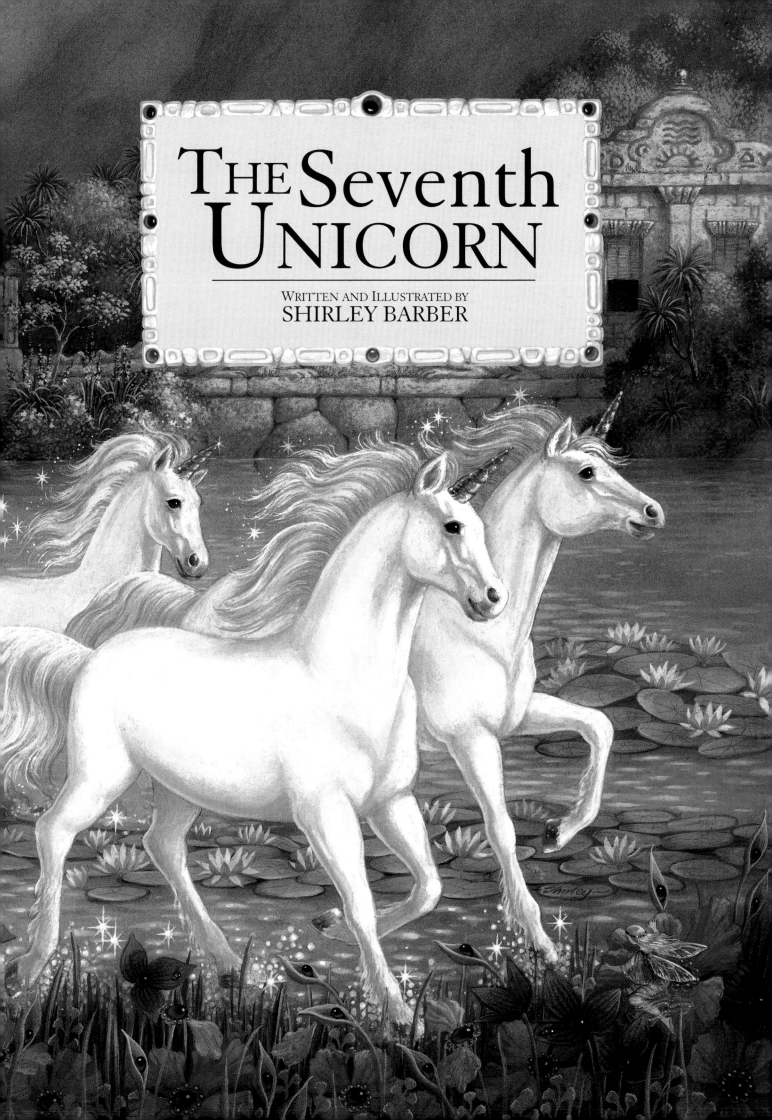

THE Seventh UNICORN

WRITTEN AND ILLUSTRATED BY
SHIRLEY BARBER

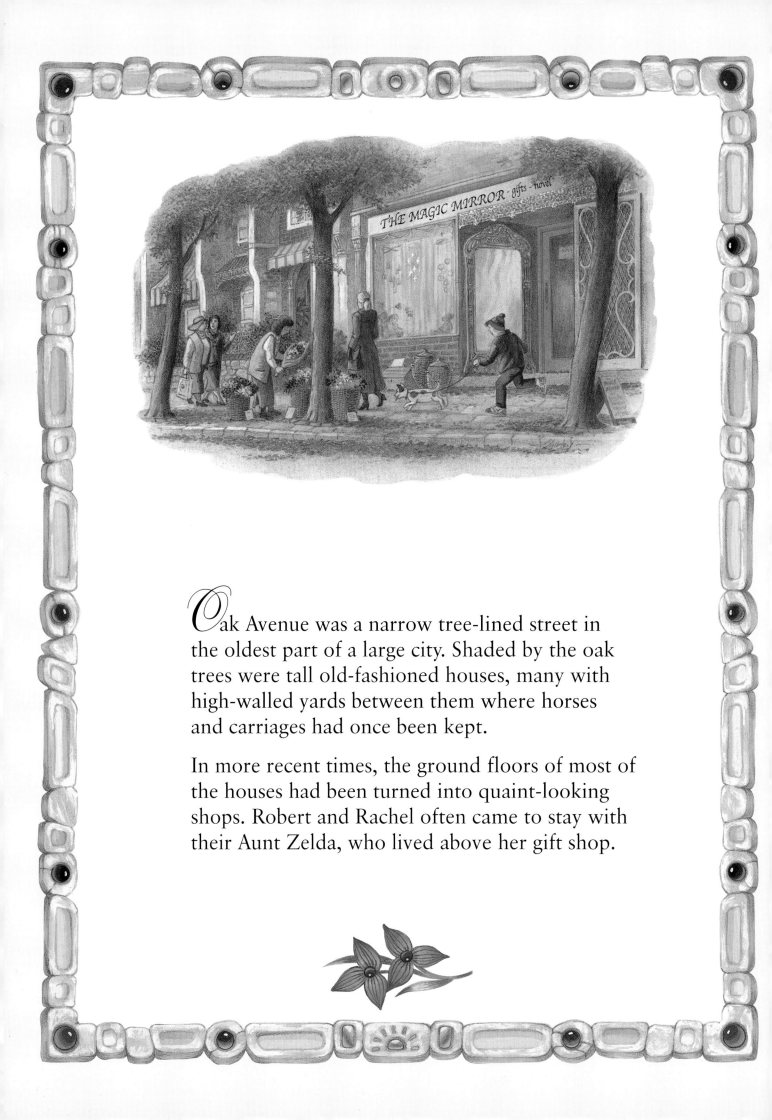

Oak Avenue was a narrow tree-lined street in the oldest part of a large city. Shaded by the oak trees were tall old-fashioned houses, many with high-walled yards between them where horses and carriages had once been kept.

In more recent times, the ground floors of most of the houses had been turned into quaint-looking shops. Robert and Rachel often came to stay with their Aunt Zelda, who lived above her gift shop.

Many of the shops in Oak Avenue had names
that were easy to remember. Aunt Zelda's gift shop
was called The Magic Mirror because the first
thing you saw, right at the entrance, was a big
mirror in a strangely-carved frame. The mirror was
so old that the glass was misty and silver-speckled.
Rachel felt sure it really *was* a magic mirror.

"If you gaze into it for a long time you begin to see
a beautiful world in there, behind the silver
speckles," she said.

Robert just laughed and Aunt Zelda, closing the
barred shop door, replied, "You might see it more
clearly if you gave the mirror a good polish."

So early next morning, when the avenue was quiet
and no one was about, the children polished the mirror.

Robert was impatient to try
out a new giant slide which had been
set up in the park at the end of Oak Avenue.
So when they had finished cleaning the mirror he
ran off. Rachel was about to follow him when a
sudden movement made her glance back at the
mirror. Imagine her amazement when she saw a little
pearl-white horse leap from the mirror in a swirl of
star-dust, and trot swiftly away between the trees.
"A unicorn!" she whispered. "I'm sure it was a
real-live unicorn!"

Rachel ran to catch up to Robert.

"Oh, come on, Rachel," he scoffed, "First a magic mirror and now a unicorn!" With that he dashed into a corner store to buy a bag of his favorite candy. Rachel stood crossly looking at the gemstones in Jemima's Jewels shop window.

"I really did see a unicorn," she thought to herself.

But when Robert reappeared and gave her some candy she stopped feeling annoyed with him, and the two raced off to the park together. The giant slide was such fun that Rachel almost forgot about what she had seen until...

The Corner Shoppe

Jemima's Jewels

Special today

fresh
bread
daily

...the little white unicorn trotted into view! His horn and hooves were golden and star-dust glittered in his mane and tail. He came right up to the children, as if he wanted to play. "What did I tell you?" Rachel whispered. "Isn't he beautiful!" "Yes! And he absolutely loves candy!" laughed Robert.

The honking of a distant car-horn startled the unicorn and he suddenly wheeled in a cloud of star-dust and galloped away, his golden hooves silent on the fallen leaves.

"Let's go back and tell Aunt Zelda that her mirror really *is* magic!" said Rachel. So the children hurried back along Oak Avenue, but this time on the other side. As they were passing the high-walled yard next to The Wizard's Castle, an antique shop, Robert stopped suddenly.

"What is it?" asked Rachel. Without replying, Robert scrambled up the nearest oak tree and peered over the wall. "Rachel," he called down softly. "There are six more unicorns in there. They're all tied up, and they look very unhappy."

"Come down quickly!" hissed Rachel. "Someone's coming!" Down slid Robert, just in time.

A man had unlocked the shop door and was carrying out a strange assortment of antiques to arrange on the sidewalk. He wore a wizard's pointed hat with the name of his shop on it, and a big cloak sewn with stars, so that he looked just like a real wizard. When he went back into the shop the children sped past and up the avenue towards Aunt Zelda's gift shop.

The children were almost at Aunt Zelda's shop
when the seventh unicorn cantered past. Right
before their eyes, he leapt back into the mirror.

"Come on!" cried Robert. "Follow him!" Despite his sister's protest, Robert pulled her with him into the mirror, and they went through the glass as if it was water.

On the other side of the
mirror Rachel's nervousness
faded as she saw they had
entered a beautiful land,
strangely shadowed at the
edges but filled with
jeweled flowers
and grasses.

"Welcome to Arcadia," said a soft voice
behind them. Rachel and Robert turned
and saw a group of beautiful children.
"Or welcome to what is left of Arcadia,"
said their leader. "For see how on every
side a shadow creeps to destroy
our lovely world!"

Rachel and Robert looked
where the girl pointed. They
realized that what they had thought was a
shadow was really a creeping fog which
withered flowers and trees where it touched them.
"An evil wizard discovered the spell to open a door
into our world," continued the young Arcadian leader.
"Each day he entered through the magic mirror, bound
a unicorn with a magic halter and led it away. When he
steals our last unicorn, Arcadia will be destroyed —
only the power of seven unicorns keeps our world
whole and well. We sent our seventh unicorn
through the mirror to seek out the other six
but he could not find them."

Rachel and Robert looked at each other. *They* knew where the missing unicorns were. The wizard must have entered the magic mirror while Aunt Zelda was at the back of the shop.

The children quickly jumped through the magic mirror into the shop. Excitedly they told their amazed aunt all that had happened.

"We must work out a plan to rescue the other unicorns," she said, once she had recovered from her surprise. "We'll have to start very early in the morning before the wizard is out of bed — and we'll need a big bag of candy!"

Next morning at sunrise,
while Aunt Zelda guarded the Magic
Mirror doorway, Rachel and Robert ran down
Oak Avenue. Rachel kept a lookout for the wizard
while Robert climbed over the wall to where the
unicorns huddled miserably together. He quietly
unbolted the big gate and pulled off the magic halters,
one by one. The six unicorns silently trotted out
into the street, where Rachel gave them each
some candy. Soon the two children were
running full speed up the avenue with
the hungry unicorns following
close behind.

Aunt Zelda was anxiously waiting outside her gift shop, ready to guide the unicorns back to Arcadia. Rachel leapt through the mirror, ahead of the unicorns, and threw handfuls of candy among the jeweled flowers. The six unicorns followed her back into their own world, and began to crunch the candy.

Next came Robert and Aunt Zelda.
With cries of joy the Arcadians came
running to hug and pet their unicorns,
all seven together again at last.
Then, golden light filled the
land and the dark shadows
were driven away.

For a moment they stood watching, then Aunt Zelda drew the children back to their own world...

... only to come face to face with the furious wizard!

"Let me pass!" he thundered. "I need the power of the unicorns to be the greatest wizard in the world."

Aunt Zelda quickly snatched up a heavy candlestick and smashed the mirror into a thousand pieces!

"The door is closed now," she said. "Arcadia is safe from you forever!"

The wizard scowled horribly, then stamped back to his antique shop and slammed his door.

Aunt Zelda and the children were overjoyed that
they had saved Arcadia from the wizard. They knew
they would never forget that beautiful world as long
as they lived. The ornate mirror frame was soon
fitted with a new glass, and although it was no
longer a doorway into another world, Rachel and
Robert often gazed into it. Sometimes they could just
make out a shimmering pearly form. They were sure
it was a unicorn looking out at them — perhaps he
was thinking about candy!

The Five Mile Press Pty Ltd
950 Stud Road Rowville
Victoria 3178 Australia
Email: publishing@fivemile.com.au
www.fivemile.com.au
This edition first published 2004
Reprinted in 2005
Text and illustrations © Marbit Pty Ltd.
Cover design by Diana Vlad

National Library of Australia Cataloguing-in-Publication date
Barber, Shirley
The Seventh Unicorn
ISBN 1741243998
1. Title.
2. A823.3